Team

written by Sally Murphy

illustrated by Anna Hancock

raintree

Engage Literacy is published in 2013 by Raintree.
Raintree is an imprint of Capstone Global Library Limited, a company
incorporated in Engand and Wales having its registered office at 7 Pilgrim
Street, London, EC4V 6LB – Registered company number: 6695582
www.raintree.co.uk

Written by Sally Murphy
Lead authors Jay Dale and Anne Giulieri
Cover illustration and illustrations by Anna Hancock (The Illustrator's Agency)
Edited by Gwenda Smyth
UK edition edited by Dan Nunn, Catherine Veitch and Sian Smith
Designed by Susannah Low, Butterflyrocket Design

The Team
ISBN: 978 1 406 26544 6
10 9 8 7 6 5 4 3 2 1

Printed and bound in the United Kingdom.

Contents

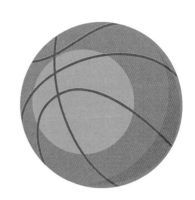

Chapter 1
Training

"Catch!" called Kelly, as she threw the basketball to her friend, Mischa. Mischa bounced the ball while Kelly ran closer to the basket.

"I'm here," called Kelly. She held her hands ready and caught the ball.

"You can do it," said Mischa. "Shoot!"

Kelly took a big breath. She crouched, looked at the goal and then pushed the ball high. It reached the edge of the basket and then dropped through.

"Goal!" shouted Kelly.

"High five!" said Mischa. "You're getting really good at shooting."

"Thanks," said Kelly. "I wish I could shoot goals like that in our real games."

"Me too," said Mischa, sadly, "but it's hard when the boys never pass the ball to us."

Kelly and Mischa were the only girls in their under-11s basketball team. They trained hard and were always at Saturday's game. But the three boys in their team never passed the ball to them. Nick, Ahmed and Michael only liked to pass to each other.

"Well," said Kelly, "all we can do is keep trying. Now, let's get to training."

UNDER-11s BASKETBALL TEAM

BACK ROW (LEFT TO RIGHT): NICK, COACH BROWN, AHMED
FRONT ROW (LEFT TO RIGHT): KELLY, MISCHA, MICHAEL

At training, Ahmed and Michael were waiting with Coach Brown. But both girls noticed that Nick wasn't there.

"I have some bad news," said Coach Brown. "Nick has broken his arm. He won't be able to play basketball for six weeks."

"Oh, no," said Michael. "We won't win any games without Nick."

Coach Brown smiled. "Well," he said, "we will just have to do our best. By the way," he continued, "we have a new player joining us. Look! Here he comes right now."

Mischa leaned towards Kelly. "Another boy," she whispered. "I wish it was a girl."

Chapter 2
Karl Joins the Team

The new boy's name was Karl. He worked hard at training. When Coach Brown told the children to run around the court to warm up, he ran very fast. When they practised dribbling the ball, he bounced it to the other end and back without dropping the ball once.

"He's very good," said Mischa to Kelly.

"Mmmm," answered Kelly. "He is."

When it was time to practise passing and catching, Ahmed and Michael passed to each other. Kelly and Mischa moved apart and started the drill.

"Can I join you?" asked Karl.

Kelly was surprised. The boys always practised together. "Oh!" she said. "Of course!"

She threw the ball to Karl. Karl passed it to Mischa who quickly passed it back to him. Karl was ready and caught the ball without a problem.

"Good catch," said Kelly, smiling.

Chapter 3
Game Day

On game day, Kelly and Mischa were surprised again. Instead of the boys only passing to each other, Karl shared the ball around. When he got the ball he passed to whoever was free. Sometimes he passed it to Ahmed or Michael, but other times he passed it to Mischa or Kelly.

Once, Karl bounced the ball to their team's end, then threw the ball to Kelly. She bounced twice, stepped around a player from the other team, and aimed at the basket. The ball went through the basket. Kelly smiled. She had scored her first goal in a **real** game.

"Well done, Kelly," called Coach Brown.

The crowd clapped and Michael patted Kelly on the back. "I didn't know you could shoot like that," he said.

When the buzzer sounded for the end of the game, Mischa looked at the scoreboard. They had won the game without Nick, their best player. She smiled at Kelly. "That was a great game," she said.

Chapter 4
Grand Final

Two weeks later, the team ran onto the court for the under-11s basketball grand final.

"We can do it, guys," said Karl, as the team came together before the game.

"Of course we can," Kelly agreed. She hoped she was right. The other team was very good.

Just then, the siren went for the game to begin.

Every time Kelly's team scored a goal, the other team scored the next one. By half-time the scores were even.

When Kelly came off the court, she was surprised to see Nick sitting next to Coach Brown. His arm was in a sling.

"I came to cheer for my team," he announced, happily. "You're playing really well," he said, smiling at Kelly.

Kelly smiled back.

Back on the court it was still a close game.
The scores were even and there wasn't
long to go. Michael had the ball. He bounced
it twice, then passed the ball to Mischa.
Mischa then passed the ball to Karl.
But Karl was too far from the goal to shoot,
so he passed it on to Ahmed.

"I'm free," called Kelly. Ahmed threw the ball
to her and she caught it, but she was a long
way from the basket.

Kelly heard a voice from the crowd cheering
her on. It was Nick. "Come on, Kelly,"
he shouted. "Shoot! You can do it!"

Kelly took a deep breath, aimed carefully
and threw. The ball soared through the air and,
just as the siren sounded, it dropped through
the hoop.

The crowd cheered!

"Yes!" Mischa punched the air. "You did it,
Kelly. We won the game."

Kelly smiled. The crowd clapped as she and her teammates shook hands with the players on the other team.

"Well done, team," beamed Coach Brown, holding the trophy in his hand. "Now gather together. I want to take a photo of the team with the trophy."

Michael, Mischa and Ahmed stood in a row. Karl and Kelly knelt in front with the trophy between them.

"Smile!" Coach Brown told them.

"Wait!" cried Kelly. "Someone is missing."
She waved at Nick, still sitting on the bench.
"Come on," she called. "You're part of this
team, too."

Nick returned Kelly's smile as he crouched next to her. "I wish I could have played, too," he said, "but I'll be back next year."

"Of course you will," Kelly replied. "With six good players, we'll each be able to have a rest off the court."

"Yes," Mischa joined in. "We can take turns."

Michael thought for a while. Then he smiled. "Yes," he agreed. "We play **so** much better when we work as a team."